The Cycle of Your Life

by Rebecca Weber

Content Adviser: September Kirby, CNS, MS, RN,
Instructor, Health Promotion and Wellness,
South Dakota State University

Reading Adviser: Rosemary G. Palmer, Ph.D.,
Department of Literacy, College of Education,
Boise State University

Spyglass
BOOKS

COMPASS POINT BOOKS

Minneapolis, Minnesota

Compass Point Books
3109 West 50th Street, #115
Minneapolis, MN 55410

Visit Compass Point Books on the Internet at *www.compasspointbooks.com*
or e-mail your request to *custserv@compasspointbooks.com*

Photographs ©: Brand X Pictures, cover, 4, 9, 16; David Falconer, 5; Clouds Hill Imaging Ltd./Corbis,
6, 8; Bruce Coleman Inc./Joe McDonald, 7; Jose Luis Pelaez, Inc./Corbis, 10, 15; Bruce Coleman Inc./
Stephen Kline, 11; Corbis, 12; Digital Vision, 13, 14, 18, 20 (bottom), 21; Stephanie Maze/Corbis, 17;
Tim Boyle/Getty Images, 19; PhotoDisc, 20 (top).

Editor: Patricia Stockland
Photo Researcher: Marcie C. Spence
Designer: Jaime Martens

Library of Congress Cataloging-in-Publication Data
Weber, Rebecca.
  The cycle of your life / by Rebecca Weber.
      p. cm. — (Spyglass books)
  Summary: Introduces the human life cycle, providing examples of various things a person can do
  as he or she reaches different stages of life.
  Includes bibliographical references and index.
  ISBN 0-7565-0625-5 (hardcover)
  1. Life cycle, Human—Juvenile literature. [1. Life cycle, Human.] I. Title. II. Series.
  QP83.8.W43 2004
  612.6—dc22   2003014480

Contents

NOTE: Glossary words are in **bold** the first time they appear.

Here You Are!

Everything that is alive on Earth is part of a life cycle. A cycle happens over and over again. You are part of a life cycle, too.

Long Life

Most people in the United
States live 77 years. The
oldest person in the world
lived 122 years!

Life Begins

A life cycle begins with a single *cell* in a woman's body. This cell is called an egg.

Sperm from a man meets with the egg cell. Then it starts to grow.

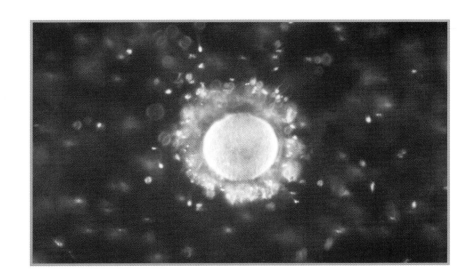

Eggs

All animals begin as eggs.
Birds and reptiles lay their eggs.
Then the baby animal hatches.
Mammal eggs grow inside a
female's body.

7

Growing Inside

Next, the egg cell splits into two cells. The cells keep splitting. They grow into body parts. These parts are a *fetus.* The fetus gets bigger.

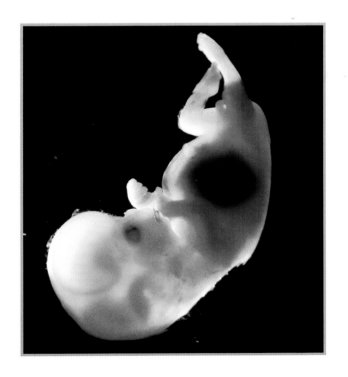

Life Inside

A fetus grows inside a woman's body. This takes about 40 weeks.

9

Time to Be Born

The fetus becomes big enough to be born. A baby needs its parents for everything. It cannot feed or clean itself. It cannot move from place to place.

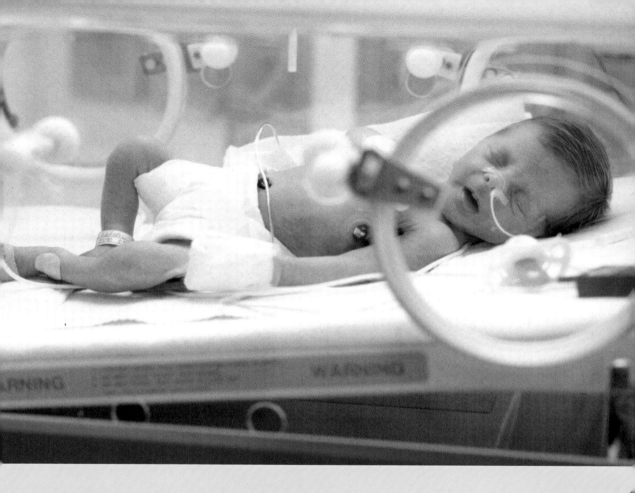

Early Babies

Some babies are born too early.
They are very small. These
babies need special care.
They stay in the hospital
until they are strong enough
to go home.

11

Getting Bigger

A baby grows into a toddler. Toddlers learn new things each day. They learn how to walk, talk, and make *decisions.*

First Years

The baby grows into a child. From ages 2 until 11, a child grows bigger and stronger. Children learn how to take care of themselves.

Growing Up

Next, a child reaches *puberty.* Humans grow to their full size from about ages 12 to 18. This is when the body prepares itself to make babies.

Big and Tall

During puberty, a body grows fast. Some kids grow as much as 4 inches (10 centimeters) a year!

The Full Cycle

Next, a person becomes an adult. Many adults start families. An adult has a child. Then the human life cycle starts over again.

Helping the Life Cycle

Each person has a life cycle.
Adoption helps a child's life cycle
keep going. Parents take care
of their adopted children.
This helps the children grow.

17

In the End

A person's life cycle ends when the person dies. Still, the life cycle goes on with the person's children and grandchildren.

Part of Life

All things that are alive die
some day. If living things
did not die, Earth would get
very crowded.

Other Life Cycles

- Sea horses have an interesting life cycle. The male sea horse carries the babies until they are ready to be born.

- Cuckoos lay their eggs in nests built by other birds. When the baby cuckoos hatch, they start kicking very hard. Soon, they have kicked out the babies of the birds who built the nest.

- Elephants in the wild help each other have babies. When a female elephant is ready to have a baby, two other females go with her. They stand guard to make sure that nothing harms her or her baby.

Glossary

adoption–the act of raising a child that was given birth by someone else and becoming its legal parent

cell–the smallest building block of any living thing

decisions–things that are decided or choices that are made

fetus–a human that has not been born yet because it is still developing body parts

mammal–an animal that grows hair and feeds its young milk

puberty–the time when a young mammal's body grows to adulthood

sperm–liquid produced by a male that can meet with a female's egg to make a baby

Learn More

Books

Douglas, Ann. *Before You Were Born: The Inside Story!* Toronto: Owl Books, 2000.

Trumbauer, Lisa. *The Life Cycle of a Dog.* Mankato, Minn.: Pebble Books, 2002.

On the Web

For more information on *The Cycle of Your Life,* use FactHound to track down Web sites related to this book.

1. Go to *www.compasspointbooks.com/ facthound*
2. Type in this book ID: 0756506255
3. Click on the *Fetch It* button. Your trusty FactHound will fetch the best Web sites for you!

Index

GR: K
Word Count: 205

From Rebecca Weber

The world is such a great place! I love teaching kids how to take care of themselves and take care of nature.